We hope you enjoy this book.
Please return or renew it by the due date.
You can renew it at **www.norfolk.gov.uk/libraries**
or by using our free library app. Otherwise you can
phone **0344 800 8020** - please have your library
card and pin ready.
You can sign up for email reminders too.

MEGAN McDONALD

illustrated by Peter H. Reynolds

JUDY MOODY

MOOD

MARTIAN

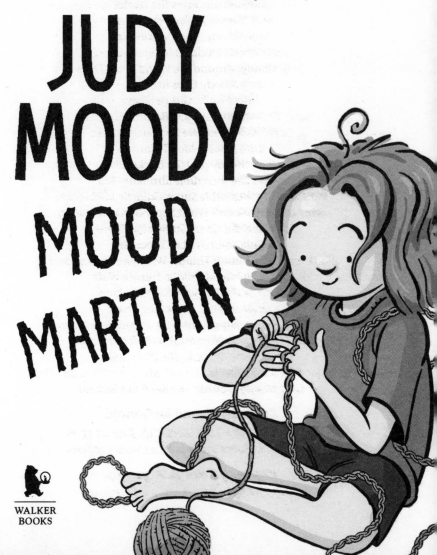

WALKER
BOOKS

First published 2015 by Walker Books Ltd
87 Vauxhall Walk, London SE11 5HJ

This edition published 2018

2 4 6 8 10 9 7 5 3 1

Text © 2014 Megan McDonald
Illustrations © 2014, 2010 Peter H. Reynolds
Judy Moody font © 2003 Peter H. Reynolds

The right of Megan McDonald and Peter H. Reynolds to be identified as
author and illustrator respectively of this work has been asserted by them
in accordance with the Copyright, Designs and Patents Act 1988

Judy Moody ™. Judy Moody is a registered trademark
of Candlewick Press Inc., Somerville MA

This book has been typeset in Stone Informal

Printed and bound in Great Britain by CPI Group (UK) Ltd, Croydon, CR0 4YY

British Library Cataloguing in Publication Data:
a catalogue record for this book
is available from the British Library

ISBN 978-1-4063-8079-8
ISBN 978-1-4063-8266-2

www.walker.co.uk

MIX
Paper from
responsible sources
FSC® C020471

For Ann Stott
M. M.

To Ethan and Kate Rosegard,
Macy and Walker Sweeny, and Billy Torres
P. H. R.

Table of Contents

In a Mood

She, Judy Moody, was in a mood. A sour-ball mood. A mad-face mood. All because school photos had come home that day.

If Stink came into her room, he would ask to see her school picture. And if he asked to see her school picture, he would see that she had been wearing her I AM GIRL, HEAR ME ROAR T-shirt. (The same one she wore today.) And if he saw her wearing her ROAR T-shirt in her school photograph, he would also see that she looked like Sasquatch. With bird's-nest hair in her face and in her eyes.

Mum and Dad were going to freak. "Just once we'd like to have a nice school photo of our girl," Dad had said just this morning.

"Maybe this will be the year," Mum had said.

But third grade was no different.

Judy spread out her school pictures on the floor. She looked like:

A one-eyed pirate
(Second grade)

A clown
(Kindergarten)

A boy
(First grade)

I AM GIRL HEAR ME ROAR

Sasquatch
(Third grade)

If only Mum and Dad would forget about school photos this year. Fat chance. Maybe Judy could pretend the dog ate them! Too bad the Moodys didn't have a dog. Only Mouse the cat. She could say that an evil school-photo bandit erased them from the master computer. Hardly.

To make things worse, Rocky had grabbed her Sasquatch picture in class and wouldn't give it back. Then he passed it to Frank, which made Judy yelp and jump up out of her seat instead of doing her maths. That's when Mr Todd said the *A* word.

Antarctica.

The desk at the back of the room where Judy had to go to chill out. For the third time that day! Never in the History of Judy had she been to Antarctica that many times in a row.

A doughnut-sized sicky spot sat in her stomach just remembering it.

That's why she, Judy Moody, was in a mood. A finger-knitting, don't-think-about-school-photographs, need-to-be-alone mood. As in *by herself.* As in no stinky little brother to bug and bother her like a pesky mosquito. *Bzzz!* Stink was always in her ear.

Judy's Number One Favourite Place to curl up with Mouse was on her top bunk, but Stink would for-sure find her there.

She crawled over gobs of flip-flops and blobs of dirty clothes to her second favourite spot to be alone – the very back of her wardrobe. She popped a wad of Stink's yard-long bubblegum in her mouth.

"Don't look at me like that, Mouse. What Stink doesn't know won't hurt him."

She picked up a skein of grey-brown wool and looped it around her thumb. Mouse batted the finger-knitting chain with her paw.

Over. Under. Over. Under. Back. Loop-de-loop-de-loop. Judy tugged on the long chain of apple-green wool that dangled from her left hand. Her fingers flew. She, Judy Moody, was the fastest finger knitter in Frog Neck Lake, Virginia. The fastest

finger knitter in the east. Probably the fastest in the whole wide world!

Finger knitting was the greatest – no knitting needles needed. She looped the wool over her fingers, one, two, three, four, back, over, under, through … just like Grandma Lou had taught her during the big blackout of Hurricane Elmer.

Judy's wardrobe was like a secret little room all to herself. It even had a window. A small, round window just like the kind they had on ships. Sailing ships. Pirate ships.

The ship sailed across the blue ocean, bobbing on the waves under a sky full of marshmallow clouds. Judy and Mouse rocked back and forth as the ship's hammock swung in the breeze. Until the ship hit a giant wave and...

Mouse overboard!

Judy tossed her chain of knitting to Mouse. She felt a tug on the line. It was—

"Stink!" Judy snapped out of her day-dream. Her gum went flying. "You scared the bubblegum out of me!"

"Where'd you get that gum?" asked Stink.

"Nowhere. It's ABC gum." She picked it up and popped it back in. "How'd you find me, anyway?"

"I followed the trail of wool."

The long, colourful chain of finger knitting snaked across the bottom of her wardrobe, climbed up and over piles of books and towers of toys, wound around Sock Mountain and crept out the door.

"Well, bad idea. I'm in a mood."

"How was I supposed to know?"

"Clues one, two and three: those

doohickeys that hang on the doorknob?"

"Oh. I thought you were going to say school photos."

"That too."

"Somebody's in a mood."

"Bingo!"

"Can I help it if I don't go around reading doorknobs?"

"I have an idea," said Judy. "Mum read me a book about Louisa May Alcott—"

"Louisa May Who?"

"She's only the most famous author of the most famous book in the world, *Little Women*."

"Cool. Is it about miniature people?

And do they live in matchboxes and take baths in thimbles and stuff? And do they know the Borrowers?"

"N-O! Anyhow, it's a known fact that Louisa May had a lot of moods. Ask anyone. So she had this sausage pillow."

"Weird."

"A sausage pillow is a long skinny pillow. When it was standing up on end it meant she was happy and in a good mood – *Come on in.* But when it was lying down on its side, hoo boy, look out – *Do not disturb,* Louisa May was in a mood."

Judy looked around and grabbed a fuzzy pillow. "See this pillow? This will be my mood pillow. It'll be our signal. If the pillow's sitting up, it means *I'm in a good*

mood. *Come on in*. But if it's lying down –
Bad mood. Go away. Much better than a
doorknob doohickey."

"But what if the pillow was standing
up and the window was open and a hurricane came and super-high winds blew
down the pillow and knocked it on its
side? Or what if a giant monster bigger
than King Kong came and picked up our
house and shook it like a toothpick and
the pillow fell over?"

"Fine." Judy plucked a marker pen
from her pencil case. She set the pillow in
her lap. On one side, she drew a happy
face for *good* mood. On the other side, she
drew a frowny face for *bad* mood.

"This will be my mood pillow. Happy

face means *Come on in.*
Frowny face means
Go away." Judy leaned
the pillow against the
wall – frowny face
out. "The pillow has
spoken, Stink."

Stink made a face. "I get it. I get it. All I really wanted was to ask if I could use your markers."

"In the pencil case, Stinkerbell."

"I'm making a T-shirt for Backwards Day tomorrow."

Backwards Day! Backwards Day was only Judy's favourite day of the whole entire year, next to April Fools' Day (her birthday) and Wear Purple for Peace Day.

Judy turned that mood pillow right around. The pillow smiled.

She had an idea for Backwards Day too. A way-good idea. A not-bad-mood idea.

Backwards Day

The next morning, Stink poked his head into Judy's room. He had his baseball cap *and* his trousers on backwards. He was singing "Boat, boat, boat your row". And he was wearing a T-shirt that said KNITS.

"Knits Moody. I like it," said Judy. She held up her finger-knitting chain. "Hey! I could teach you to finger knit, Knits Moody."

"*KNITS* is *STINK* spelled backwards," said Stink.

"Luck-y!" said Judy. "I wish my backwards name was Knits." She was searching for a hairbrush. That was clue number one about her Backwards Day idea.

"Hey, Judy. What has four legs and goes *oom oom*?"

"A hungry zebra?" Judy guessed.

"N-O! A cow on Backwards Day!"

Judy cracked up. "That's funny, Knits."

"Really? You mean it? Thanks! You never like my jokes."

Pretending to like Stink's joke was clue number two.

Stink ran to his room and came back with his yardstick of bubblegum. "Here. You can have this. There's seven centimetres of gum left."

"Really?"

"For letting me use your markers. And for laughing at my joke." Stink ran downstairs.

Clue number three: Judy peeled off her I AM GIRL, HEAR ME ROAR T-shirt and stuck it in her bottom drawer, then took her time choosing what to wear. When she was dressed, she checked herself out in the mirror. Once. Twice. Three times. *Mirror, mirror, on the wall. Who's the most backwards of them all?*

Then Judy ran downstairs to grab her lunch.

Mum's jaw dropped when she saw Judy. "Star-spangled bananas!"

"Great Caesar's ghost!" said Dad.

"What's with your hair?" asked Stink. "Are you Cleopatra or something?"

"Nope. Don't you get it?" Judy twirled around so her family could get the full effect.

Her hair was not a bird's-nest mess. It was brushed – not one single bit Sasquatch. It was held back with real-and-actual kirby grips that would have made Nancy Drew, Girl Detective, proud. Judy's clothes matched. Not a tiger stripe in sight. Not even a shark. Even her socks and shoes matched. And she wore only one watch.

"Let me guess," cried Stink. "You're Jessica Finch. Wait. I don't get it. How is that backwards?"

"I'm the opposite of me, Stink."

"You look great, honey," said Mum. "Thank you for brushing your hair."

"I hardly know my own daughter," said Dad.

"You're backwards every day, so on Backwards Day, you're normal?" Stink asked.

"Something like that," said Judy. She held out her mood-ring hand. "Check it out. I painted it with purple nail polish. My mood ring will remind me to be in a good mood all day."

"Judy Goody-Goody," said Stink.

"Good for you," said Mum.

"You kids don't want to be late for the sub," said Dad.

"Huh?" said Stink.

"Very funny, Dad. *Sub* is backwards for *bus*, Stink." Judy ran out the door to the sub, holding her kirby grips in place.

❀   ❀   ❀

When Judy and Rocky got to Class 3T, there was no Class 3T. It was Class 3D. The sign on the door now said: MR DDOT'S ROOM. When they stepped inside, Mr Todd's desk was at the back of the room. The guinea pigs were at the front of the room. And the alphabet on the notice-board started with a *Z*! A strange sentence was scribbled on the blackboard. *MR OWL ATE MY METAL WORM.* Weird!

"Hey, Moody. Hey, Zang. What do you think?" asked Mr Todd.

"Why are you calling me Zang?" asked Rocky.

"Calling us by our last names is backwards!" said Judy. "Right, Mr Todd?"

"And I'm Mr Ddot for today." Mr Todd chuckled. He was wearing a shirt with polka dots. And his tie was on wrong. "How do you like my tie?"

"Weird and weirder," said Rocky.

"Moody," said Mr Todd. "Something's different."

"My hair's brushed and my clothes match and everything!" said Judy.

"Backwards looks good on you," said Mr Todd.

Frank had his clothes on inside out. Even his backpack was inside out. Jessica

Finch's ponytail stood straight up in the air. "And I'm *not* wearing pink," she said.

Amy Namey sat down next to Judy. She was wearing glasses on the back of her head. "Mr Todd said I could be in your class today."

"Backwards!" said Judy.

Backwards Day was the best! Breaktime came first instead of after lunch.

In Spelling, they had to spell all the words backwards. Judy's word was racecar. "*Racecar.* R-A-C-E-C-A-R." The room got super quiet. "Wait a second. It's the same backwards AND forwards," said Judy. "You tricked me!" Everybody cracked up.

"It's called a palindrome," said Mr Todd.

"Can anybody else think of a word that's spelled the same backwards and forwards? Pearl?"

"*Pop,*" said Frank.

"*Namey?*"

"*Toot,*" said Amy.

"*Graff?*"

"*Hannah,*" said Hannah. Everybody cracked up more.

"Very good," said Mr Todd. He pointed to the strange sentence on the board. *MR OWL ATE MY METAL WORM.* Jessica Finch raised her hand.

"Finch?"

"The whole sentence is the same backwards and forwards!" said Jessica.

"Wow. You figured that out so fast!" said Judy. Being extra nice to Jessica Finch was backwards too.

In Maths, Mr Todd gave them answers, and they had to figure out the questions. And in Silent Reading, they did not even have to be silent.

Class 3D-not-3T walked down the corridor backwards to the art room. All the art was hanging upside down! Then, they got to lie on the floor and draw on paper taped to the bottom of their desks.

At lunch, Judy sat with her friends. Jessica Finch came over with her hot lunch. "Your lunch is backwards," Judy said. "It's breakfast!"

Rocky, Frank and Amy opened their lunch boxes. Rocky looked at Frank. Frank looked at Amy. Amy looked at Judy.

"Don't be mad," said Frank.

Judy glanced at her mood ring. Purple. She remembered she was not going to get in a mood. "Why would I be mad?"

"Cheese strings," said Rocky and Amy at the same time.

"Why would anybody be mad about cheese strings?" Jessica asked.

"You don't know about the Cheese-String Incident of Last Week?" Rocky asked. "See, Frank and Amy and I always have cheese strings. We like to bend them and pull them apart and make stuff like cheese catapults."

"And plait them sometimes," said Amy. "And make bracelets."

"Judy got in a mood because her food was no fun," said Rocky.

"I never get cheese strings," said Judy.

"So one day last week, Judy grabbed my cheese string," said Frank. "It flew halfway across the cafeteria. A kid slipped on it and Judy got in trouble with the Thursday Lunch Lady."

"Everybody knows Thursday Lunch Lady is scary," said Jessica.

"Hello! It's Backwards Day. I'm doing everything backwards, so I am NOT going to get in a mood about cheese strings. I am not going to get in a mood *all day.*"

"All day?" said Rocky.

"The whole day?" said Amy and Frank.

"All day. The whole day."

"Phew," said Rocky.

"Phew," said Amy and Frank.

"Is that why you were nice to me in Spelling?" Jessica asked. Judy just smiled.

Judy's friends took out their cheese strings.

Jessica pulled a pink straw from her backpack. "It's a Magic Straw. It turns plain white milk into pink strawberry milk, like magic."

"Rare," said Judy. She pulled the string on the edge of her boring old baloney. She sipped her boring old not-magic milk. But she did *not* get in a mood. If only she had some wool. Some green-with-envy finger-knitting yarn.

In the playground, Judy wanted to skip backwards, but she was afraid it might mess up her kirby-gripped hair. In the classroom, she organized her desk. Books on the left, notebooks on the right. She made a folder for IN-CLASS WORK and a folder for HOMEWORK. She even made some Grouchy pencils UN-Grouchy. When she was done, she emptied the pencil sharpener without being asked.

She did not let herself get in a bad mood all day. She did not call Jessica "Fink-Face Finch". Not even when Jessica got three whole Third-Grade Rock Star stickers. Judy did not go to Antarctica, not even once!

Judy's mood ring stayed purple all day. The whole day. A spot of nail polish peeled off and Judy could tell that it was purple underneath. For real!

At the end of the day, Mr Todd said, "Great job today, Judy. Keep up the good work. And the good moods!" She earned three Good Work tickets. That would buy three Peace, Love and Third Grade stickers. Or a peace sign pencil!

She, Judy Moody, was the First Lady of Backwards Day, Queen of the Good Mood. In fact, Backwards

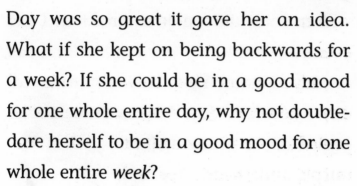

Day was so great it gave her an idea. What if she kept on being backwards for a week? If she could be in a good mood for one whole entire day, why not double-dare herself to be in a good mood for one whole entire *week*?

It would be like a contest. A stay-out-of-Antarctica contest with herself. A game, a quiz, a mini world record that only she knew about.

A secret with Me, Myself and I.

One thing was for sure and absolute

positive – it was not going to be easy-Parcheesi. So, just in case she flunk-flub-failed, she would not tell anybody.

Not even Rocky. Not even Frank. Definitely not Stink.

If nobody knew, nobody could say I told you so. Her friends, her parents and her teachers were going to be A-plus amazed.

Look out, world. Meet the new-and-improved, NOT-moody Judy!

The Jessica Experiment

If she, Judy Moody, was going to be in a good mood for one whole entire week, she was going to need info. As in hints. Tips. Ideas.

On the bus ride home, Judy asked her friends, "Hey, guys. What puts you in a good mood?"

"When I do a really good magic trick, like the Fake Finger trick," said Rocky. He pulled his index finger, pretending to yank it off. "If everybody claps and is amazed, it puts me in a good mood."

"Uh-huh." Judy scribbled a Note to Self.

"I get in a good mood when I'm done with my homework," said Frank.

"Uh-huh, uh-huh." Judy looked at her notes.

Next it was Amy's turn. "Writing stories puts me in a good mood. I dream stuff up and make it into a book and illustrate it."

Judy scribbled some more. She looked at her notes.

1. Magic trick

2. Homework

3. Write a story

"I can do this," said Judy.

"Do what?" asked Amy.

"Do what?" asked Rocky and Frank.

"Um ... nothing. Never mind."

Judy ran home and took out her list. *Magic trick.* She tried a magic card trick on Stink. But all she did was spill the pack of cards everywhere. *Homework.* Judy did not see how homework would put her in a good mood. She crossed it off the list. *Write a story.* Judy tried to write a story.

Once upon a time
It was a dark and stormy night
Pete and Repeat were sitting on the top bunk. Pete fell off. Who was left? Repeat. Pete and Repeat were sitting on the top bunk...

This story could go on and on and on. What a lemonhead! Writing a story was so *not* putting her in a good mood. Who else could she get ideas from? Mum? Dad? Stink?

It had to be somebody smart and somebody who never got sent to Antarctica.

Wait just a ding-dong minute! What

could be more perfect than to talk to Little Miss Perfect? Somebody who brushed her hair every day and followed all the rules and got good grades and had never even been *near* Antarctica.

Somebody who had a *happy* Magic 8 Ball.

Jessica A-plus Finch! Of course!

Judy could learn the facts about doing everything right all the time. Being perfect was sure to put her in a good mood. All she had to do was study her subject. Like a science experiment!

She grabbed her notebook and hopped on her bike and pedalled down the street and around the corner to Jessica Finch's house.

Ding-dong! Judy rang the bell. Jessica A-not-Aardwolf opened the door.

"Judy Moody? What are you doing here?"

She could not tell Jessica Tell-All Finch her secret. Then the whole world would know. "I, um, thought we could hang out," said Judy.

"But you never want to hang out."

"Never say never," said Judy, pushing past Jessica. "Can I come in?"

"You are in," said Jessica.

"Well, um, how about if I come up to your room?"

"Sure," said Jessica. "I was just going to start measuring things for Measure Up!, our new maths unit."

"But that doesn't start till Thursday," said Judy.

"I like to get a head start," said Jessica.

Judy perched on the edge of the bed next to Jessica. She bounced up and down, testing out the jump factor.

"My mum doesn't like me to bounce on the bed," said Jessica.

"Check," said Judy. She scribbled DO NOT BOUNCE ON BED in her notebook. Judy stared sideways at Jessica. Her hair was brushed back into a very neat ponytail and she was wearing pink. Judy wrote PUT HAIR IN PONYTAILS and WEAR PINK in her notebook.

"Why are you staring at me?" asked Jessica. "It's rude."

"No reason," said Judy. She looked around. The bed was made and there were a hundred million fluffy pink pillows on it. Stuffed-animal pigs were lined up in a row on the dressing-table. So was a piggy-bank collection.

No books or clothes were on the floor. No arts-and-crafts supplies were on the floor. No gum wrappers were on the floor. A pink robot poster on the wall said OBEY. It was creepy, but Judy didn't say so.

"Your floor is very neat," said Judy. "I can see the rug."

"Thanks," said Jessica. "I like my room clean. It puts me in a good mood."

"Check." Judy wrote *CLEAN ROOM* in her notebook.

"Why are you writing stuff down?" asked Jessica.

"No reason," said Judy, sniffing the air. "I smell cupcakes. Do you smell cupcakes?"

Jessica cackled. "That's my lip gloss." She flipped open a teeny-tiny pink plastic cupcake. Inside was gooey lip stuff. Judy tried some. Yum, yum! Maybe cupcake lip gloss was another key to a good mood. Judy wrote down *WEAR CUPCAKE LIP GLOSS.*

"You like smiley faces, huh?" In Jessica's room, Judy saw a smiley-face pillow, pencil holder and paper clips. She saw smiley-face sunglasses and slippers. Even a smiley-face mobile hung over

Jessica's desk. She picked up Jessica's smiley-face Magic 8 Ball. "Can I try?"

Jessica nodded.

Judy had a burning question. But it was a secret. So she asked herself the question silently. *Will I be able to stay in a good mood for one whole week?*

She shook the Happy 8 Ball. *Nice out-fit.* She asked the question and shook it again. *Your breath is so minty!* She tried again. *You smell great.*

"It keeps telling me that I smell great," said Judy.

"It's the lip gloss." Jessica nodded know-ingly. "Want to do homework now?"

Judy wrote *DO HOMEWORK ON TIME* in her notebook.

Jessica got out her Positively Pink see-through ruler. She got out her Positively Pink tape measure. She even had a Positively Pink yardstick.

"Wow. You have a yardstick? I have a yardstick of bubblegum. It's this long." Judy stretched out her arms. "Well, it used to be. There's actually only seven centimetres of gum left. But the box is a yard-long ruler – for real! And it has jokes and—"

"I wouldn't use it for homework if I were you," said Jessica.

Judy looked around for something to measure. "Do you have a cat? We could measure stuff like the cat's tail!" said Judy.

Jessica crinkled her forehead. "I was just going to measure the carpet." She started to stretch the tape measure across the rug. Bor-ing!

This being in a good mood was harder than it looked. Judy's fingers itched.

If only she were back in her wardrobe with her finger knitting.

She stared at Jessica some more. "Do you ever miss the bus to school?" Judy asked.

Jessica wrinkled her forehead again. "Why would I do that?"

"I mean, are you ever late to school? Say you slept late. Or read your book under the covers when you should have been getting ready. Or didn't do your Spelling homework and decided to stay home ill."

"I always do my Spelling homework. I never fake being ill. And I have a Walkie Clockie," said Jessica. She pulled an alarm clock with wheels from her bedside table. "It beeps like a robot and jumps off my bedside table when it's time to get up. I have to get out of bed to chase it around."

"Can I try?" asked Judy.

"Sure." Jessica set the clock to go off in one minute. They waited. They waited some more.

Eep! Beep! Walkie Clockie leaped to the floor. *"Out of bed, sleepyhead."* It zoomed across the carpet. *"Up and at 'em, madam!"* It zoomed under the bed. *"Rise and shine,*

friend of mine!" Judy chased it all around Jessica's room.

"Wow!" said Judy. "It walks. It talks. It rhymes. It chimes." She wrote down *GET WALKIE CLOCKIE SO I'M NEVER LATE* in her notebook. "That was fun. Let's do it again. This time—"

"It's not really a game," said Jessica. She put the clock back on her bedside table. "C'mon, let's do our homework."

Judy looked at her to-do list. She had a lot to do if she was going to stay out of Antarctica. She had a lot to learn about being in a good mood. "I can't," said Judy. "I have to – um – go finish my science experiment."

"Science experiment?" Jessica sat up straight. Her eyes got wide. "What science experiment? We don't have any—"

But Judy was already down the stairs and halfway out the front door.

Yippee skippy!

Spaghetti Yeti

First things first. As soon as Judy got home, she pulled her hair back into two Jessica Finch ponytails. Then she cleaned up her room like a friend without an R. F-I-E-N-D, spelling word No. 23 on Mr Todd's home-work list. Definition: maniac. She huffed and puffed, picking up books and games and art supplies and stuffed animals. Yawn-o-rama. Mouse watched her every move. She huffed and puffed more putting away T-shirts and shorts and socks and pyjamas. Bor-ing times two!

Mouse pounced on a sock. "Give it. It's not playtime, Mouse. I wish."

She even tossed her finger knitting into the wardrobe.

Jessica Finch was cuckoo-for-coconuts if she thought cleaning your room could put you in a good mood.

Next Judy did her this-week homework. Read, read, read. Spell, spell, spell. Multiply. Divide. Done!

Doing her homework on time did not put her in a good mood.

"Now what, Mouse?" Judy asked. She checked her notebook. Eureka! She, Judy Moody, had an idea.

Judy dug and dug like a badger to the very back of her wardrobe. She pulled out her last-year Christmas presents. Under the hand-knitted dancing mouse jumper from Grandma Lou was a present from Nana and Gramps in California. It was not a way-cool Make-Your-Own Gum kit. It was not a way-cool Make-Your-Own Seashell Night-Light kit. It was a Make-Your-Own Lip Gloss kit! Candyfloss, chocolate, *cupcake*!! Double exclamation point!!

Last Christmas, Judy would not have been caught dead wearing smelly lip gloss. But that was before the Jessica experiment. She had to try it now – in the name of good moods.

Judy did not want to mess up her clean room, so she messed up the bathroom instead. Warm water, sticky hands, smelly flavour and ... *voilà*! Cupcake lip gloss.

Mww! Mww! Mww! Judy looked in the mirror and smacked her lips. *Yum, yum.* She licked her lips. Oops. Now she needed more lip stuff. *Smack, smack, smack.* Lip-smacking good! Cupcake lip stuff *did* put her in a bit of a better mood. Who knew?

Judy went back to her room. *Sing a song of tuna fish!* Her finger-knitting chain snaked and snarled out the wardrobe door, up, over and around the doorknob, across the dressing-table and onto the floor, where Mouse was curled up sleeping on a heap of it.

Judy tugged an end out from under Mouse. "Who yarn bombed my clean room, Mouse?" she said. "Don't even try to say it was Stink."

At last, she had time for her new rave – finger knitting. She went to her wardrobe to get some more wool. But there was no more wool. Not one ball. Not one skein. Not even a snippet. She was O-U-T *out*.

Judy ran downstairs. "Mum! Mum! Can we go to Bullseye? It's a wool emergency!"

"Sorry, honey," said Mum. "All this wool costs money. Let's wait and ask

Grandma Lou for some wool next time we see her."

"But...!" Judy was about to say it was so not fair. Judy was about to say she could not wait. Judy was about to stomp up the stairs. But that would mean she was in a mood. Not a good mood. A bad mood.

Judy dashed back upstairs. Her frowny-face mood pillow glared at her.

It was only GMD No. 1, Good Mood Day Number One. Judy had to be stomp-free for the rest of the week. This being in a good mood all the time sure was not as easy-peasy, mac-and-cheesy as it looked.

Judy went badgering in her wardrobe again. She pulled out the hand-knitted dancing mouse jumper from Grandma Lou. The mouse had fluffy ears and a fluffy tummy and a fluffy tail. Judy pulled at the pink fluff. Oops! Look at that. A thread came loose.

She glanced at the door to make sure no one was watching. She pulled at the thread some more. Pull and tug and pull some more and before she knew it, the jumper was not a jumper. It was a spaghetti mess of W-O-O-L *wool*!

Just what she needed. *Knit, knit, knit.* She had to work fast before Mum or rat fink Stink found out. Judy turned her pillow around to Smiley Face.

Her chain got a little longer and a little longer. It sneaked and snaked out into the hallway now. But she was out of wool again in no time flat.

She climbed the stairs to the attic. Maybe she'd find some old wool there. *Pfff.* Cobweb city! She tore through dusty old bags and boxes and bundles.

Eureka! A stash of wool odds and ends. *Knit, knit. Loop-de-loop.* She was back in her room finger knitting up a storm when Stink came in, hands behind his back.

"Guess what I have," said Stink.

"A toad?"

"Nope."

"A cookie?"

"Nope."

"I give up."

"It's something in the sea," said Stink.

"An octopus?"

"Yes! How'd you know?" Stink brought his hands out from behind his back. He had long tentacles on his fingers.

"Cool octopus fingers," said Judy.

"*Squid* fingers," said Stink. "Wanna play Super Squid Attacks Japan? I'll be Super Squid and you can be Manta Ray. Or Tooth Fish. Or Creepy Eel."

"How about Electric Eel?" Judy asked.

"Sure."

"No, thanks. I'm finger knitting."

"We could play Spider-Man," said Stink. "I could be Doc Ock. Doctor Octopus. You could be … somebody in a bad mood."

"I'm not in a mood, Stink. I'm happy as Larry."

"Who's Larry?"

"A guy who's happy? I don't know. It's a saying, Stink. Never mind. I'm happy as a hermit crab."

"You're still a crab. Even your pillow's in a mood." Stink pointed to the frowny face.

"Must have been King Kong," said Judy. "It *was* on the smiley side, I swear!"

Judy had an idea. "How about I show

you how to finger knit and you can make a chain and we'll add it to my chain and—"

"Bor-ing!" said Stink. "Knitting is for old ladies."

"*Finger* knitting isn't," said Judy. "Finger knitting is way-cool. If I knit a super-duper long chain, I can yarn bomb the house. Or the car. Or Virginia Dare School!"

Stink perked up. "Yarn bomb?"

"You wrap the chain around some-thing outside – like the seesaw at the playground or a flagpole at school or that Virginia Dare statue in the park."

"I Virginia-Dare you to do *that*!" said Stink.

"OK, so not the statue, but maybe a park bench."

"I'm in," said Stink.

Before you could say Super Squid, Stink was loop-de-looping wool up, over and around his tentacle fingers. Judy kept knitting. Mouse batted a ball of wool around the room.

"I think I've got the hang of it," said Stink. He held out his hands. *Cat's cradle!* The wool tangled up and over and around his tentacles in one big yarn yuck.

"Super Squid is not the best at this," said Judy.

Stink cracked up. "So? Who ever heard of a squid that can knit?" *Pop! Pop! Pop, pop, pop!* He pulled off his tentacles. That's when he noticed something strange about Judy's room. Books were lined up on the shelves. Erasers were in a jar. Even Jaws was wearing a hair ribbon. "Hey, your room is weird."

"Is not."

"Is too."

"It's just neat, Stink. I cleaned it up."

"Oh, did Mum and Dad make you?" Stink asked.

"Nobody made me," said Judy.

"Then why did you clean your room?"

"No reason."

Stink picked up a few balls of wool and started to juggle. "By the way, your hair's weird too," said Stink.

"They're called ponytails," said Judy. She checked her ponytails in the mirror. "I'm going to wear them for School Photo Make-Up Day."

Stink dropped one of the balls of wool. Mouse pounced on it. Stink sat on Judy's bottom bunk. Judy picked up her finger knitting and climbed up to the top bunk. *Knit, knit, knit.* She did not say a word.

"Aren't you going to tell me to get off your bed?" Stink asked.

"You can sit there if you want," Judy told him. "It's a free country."

"Free country, huh?" Stink kept juggling. He started to hum. He hummed the "If You're Happy and You Know It" song. He hummed the "Nouns and Verbs Rap Song".

Finally, he couldn't stand it any more. "Aren't you going to tell me to stop humming? And juggling? Aren't you going to call me your little *bother* and say I'm a pest and tell me you have to do homework?"

"I did my homework."

"WHAT? You did homework *before* dinner?"

"It's not against the law to do homework."

"It's against the Law of Judy," said Stink.

He ran to get a torch and shone it in Judy's eyes. "Who are you, anyway?" Stink asked. "Why is your hair all funny and why are your lips all shiny and what's with looking in the mirror all the time? What have you done with my sister?"

"Stink, get that thing out of my eyes!"

"Imposter! Fakester! Fraudster!" Stink squealed. "Where's your pod? Did you come to Earth on a space flower?"

Judy could no-way *not-ever* tell Stink her good-mood secret. Instead she said, "Yes, Stink. I'm a clone. And you're next."

"I want my sister back. The NOT-homework-doing sister with the messy hair and the messy room and—" Stink stopped in his tracks. He sniffed the air.

His super sniffer smelled something. Some-thing strange. Something sickly sweet, like candy.

"Do you smell ... cupcakes?" Stink asked.

"It's my lip gloss," said Judy.

"AAGH!" yelled Stink. "Invasion of the body snatchers! I'm telling Mum."

Stink ran downstairs. Judy sat on the top step and eavesdropped while Stink told Mum and Dad all the ways that she was acting weird. He told Mum and Dad that the real Judy had been snatched by Pod People. He told them that the person pre-tending to be his sister was really a clone.

"Maybe we should clone *you*," Mum said. "If it means you'll clean your room."

"Hardee-har-har!" Judy heard Stink say. "This is no joke."

"I did notice she cleaned Mouse's litter tray without being told," said Mum.

"And she borrowed my tape measure and didn't even break it," said Dad. "Maybe our girl's growing up."

"Ugh!" said Stink.

Judy tiptoed back to her room and gasped. Red wool. Yellow wool. Blue wool. Pink wool. Green wool. Wool, wool everywhere! Judy's room was one big giant spider's web. Her rug looked like King Kong's plate of spaghetti.

"AARGH!" she cried.

Stink came running upstairs. "Who did this? You and your pod-people pals?"

"Not unless our cat's an extraterrestrial," said Judy. "Here, kitty, kitty. Or should I say knitty, knitty?" She pulled the guilty Mouse out from under her bunk beds, where she had been playing football with a ball of red-and-green wool.

"She looks like a Christmas stocking!" said Stink, pointing and laughing.

"Not funny, Stink." Judy held up the empty bag. "This was all the wool I had for finger knitting. Now it's one big jumbo jumble. And my room is … Planet Spaghetti."

"Cool," said Stink. "It's like a Yarn Yeti lives here. Let's do my room next."

"Stink! Did you not hear me? It's going to take a year to untangle this."

Judy felt a roar coming on. Her eyes went big. Her cheeks got puffy. Her face turned red. But she, Judy Moody, had to stop it in its tracks. She could not get in a mood about the Yarn Yeti, no matter how abominable it was. Whatever she did, she could not say *roar*.

"Meow," said Judy.

Weird, Weirder, Weirdest

That night, Judy tried to finger knit before she went to sleep. But her wool was one big spaghetti monster with no beginning and no end. It had more arms than an octopus, more legs than a clutter of spiders, more knots than a kindergartener's shoelace.

She turned off the light and wriggled under the covers on her top bunk. Out of habit, she felt for the warm spot where Mouse usually slept. Empty. Then she remembered she'd made Mouse sleep in Stink's room tonight.

At last she fell asleep. She dreamed of spaghetti. She dreamed of spider's webs. She dreamed of a Spaghetti Yeti caught in a spider's web.

When she woke up the next morning, her hair was a Super Snarl just like the wool on the floor. Judy spat on her hand and tried to tame her wild hair.

She stared at the Yarn Yeti on the floor. She picked at a scab on her knee. She thought about her knotty problem. How was she going to finger knit with this mess?

EUREKA! She, Judy Moody, had a brainwave. All it was going to take was every friend she had.

Judy turned her mood pillow to the smiley side. She hopped out of bed and pulled on a pink-ish hoodie. She slipped on her purple-all-the-time mood ring. Judy was in-the-pink and ready for GMD No. 2. Good Mood Day Number Two.

❧   ❧   ❧

At the bus stop, Rocky took one look at Judy and asked, "What's with you?"

"Nothing."

"Something's different," said Rocky, studying her.

"Ponytails," Stink told Rocky.

"My hair is brushed. I'm wearing pink." Judy fluttered her fingers. "And I used smiley-face stickers for nail polish."

"And ... you're not wearing any

84

Band-Aids. And you haven't said ROAR for like one whole day."

One day? It felt more like two years. "So?"

"So, it's weird."

"Yeah, weird," said Stink. "Invasion-of-the-Body-Snatchers weird."

"I mean, it's not even Backwards Day any more," Rocky pointed out, "but you're still backwards or something."

"Or something," said Judy.

"*And* she smells like cupcakes," Stink added.

Rocky took a whiff. "Vanilla or chocolate?" he asked.

"Red velvet," said Judy.

֍   ֍   ֍

All day, Judy's friends thought she was acting strange. When it was time to line up for a band concert, Judy let Jessica Finch go first. When Mr Todd did not call on her in Maths Lightning Round, she did not even make a face. And when they did not serve mini ice-cream sandwiches for Wednesday lunch, Judy just said, "Fruit, please."

At breaktime, a fourth grader called her a name.

"She's going to roar," said Rocky.

"She's going to roar," said Frank and Amy.

Judy drummed her fingers on her leg. She scratched an itch behind her ear. But Judy did not roar. She said, "Sticks and

stones may break my bones and all that."
Then she walked away.

"Watch this," Rocky told Frank. Amy and Jessica watched too. "Hey, Judy," called Rocky. "Let's play Four Square."

"Can't," said Judy. "I don't want to get chalk all over me."

"How about Helicopter?" asked Frank.

"Hello! My hair! It'll get all messed up."

"She's backwards, all right," said Frank.

"And it's not even Backwards Day," said Amy.

"Told you," said Rocky.

"Weird," said Frank.

"Weirder," said Amy.

"Weirdest," said Jessica Finch.

Jessica Finch pointed out that Judy was wearing pink. And ponytails. "What's that thing you always say? Same-same?" she asked.

"Hey, she's right! You guys are twins!" said Frank.

"Are you ill or something?" Rocky asked.

"Yeah, are you *sure* you're feeling OK?" asked Amy.

"Guys," said Judy, "I'm not ill. Yeti's honour." Judy crossed her heart. "Tell you what. I have an idea."

"Phew!" said Rocky. "She has an idea. Boy am I glad to hear you say that."

"What are we gonna do?" asked Frank. "Break a record? Save the world? Predict the future?"

"Have our own spelling bee?" asked Jessica Finch.

"How about that Boston tub party thing you guys did?" said Amy.

"Nope, nope, nope," said Judy. "It's something we've never done before."

"Ooh," said Amy. "What is it?"

"It's a secret," said Judy. "Come over after school and I'll tell you then."

"A Judy Moody wacky idea?" said Rocky.

"This is gonna be good," said Frank.

"This is gonna be big," said Rocky.

"Be there or be square and don't forget to brush your hair," said Judy.

"I'm in!" said Rocky.

"Me too," said Amy and Frank.

"Me three," said Jessica Finch.

Rocky pulled Judy aside. "You invited Jessica *Finch*?" he whispered. "For real?"

"It's the new me," said Judy.

Nanu Nanu

Before Judy's friends got to her house, she shoved piles and piles of her lacy finger-knitting chain into her wardrobe and shut the door. This way her room would look neat and clean à la Jessica Clean-Room Finch. Now the only thing out of place was the tangled mangle of wool made by Mouse. But thanks to her friends, that mess would be solved in no time.

When everybody got to her house, they

tried to guess what wild and crazy idea Judy had come up with this time.

"I bet we're going to make the Eiffel Tower out of icing," said Amy.

"I bet we're going to build a pyramid out of jelly," said Frank.

"I bet we're going to prank Stink with Judy's periscope," said Rocky.

"Nothing like that," said Judy.

"We're just glad you had one of your crazy ideas," said Rocky. "It means you're back."

"Back from where?"

"Never mind," said Rocky. "Just tell us what the thing is."

Judy led them up the stairs. Her mood pillow was propped against the door, smiley face out. She flung open the door to her room. *"Ta da!"* she called.

Rocky froze. Frank gaped. Jessica blinked. Amy took off her glasses and put them back on, like she wasn't seeing right. Judy's room was as neat as a pin. But right smack-dab in the middle of the floor was a giant puddle of wool. A muddle of wool. One big humongous mess of tangled-up wool!

"Welcome to Wool-a-Palooza!" Judy said eagerly.

"Wool-a-pa-whatta?" asked Jessica.

"We're going to have a wool party! Our mission, should we choose to accept the dare – which we will – is to untangle this Yarn Yeti."

"*This* is your big idea?" Frank asked.

"You're from another planet if you think this is fun," said Rocky.

"Zzzzzzz," said Amy, pretending to snore.

"I'll help!" yelped Jessica Finch, picking up a thread of pink wool.

"C'mon, you guys. It'll be fun, I promise," Judy told them.

"About as much fun as … watching socks dry," said Frank.

"Then you guys think of an idea," said Judy. "In the meantime, Frank, hold out your arms."

"Why me?" Frank asked as he held out his arms. Judy pulled at the big mess until she found an end. She started to wind the wool around Frank's hands. She wrapped and wrapped the wool in a circle. Green wool turned into blue wool, which turned into red wool.

"Can I put my hands down yet?" asked Frank. "My arms are killing me."

"Not yet," said Judy. "Hey, did you guys know a ball of wool is called a *clew*?"

"So you're *clew*-less?" asked Rocky.

"Get a clew," said Judy. She cracked herself up.

"Hey, I know. Let's play *Clue*do!" said Amy.

"Or ... I know a level-three spelling game we could play," said Jessica.

Rocky flared his nostrils. "Count me out," he said. "Let's be detectives again."

"We could solve a real-life mystery," said Frank. "You know, like we did when that puppy, Mr Chips, went missing!"

"Great!" said Judy. Her friends smiled and nodded, eager to hear what the mystery was going to be. "I have an idea..."

"Quiet, everybody," hissed Rocky. "Judy's getting one of her brainwaves."

Judy held a bright-idea finger in the air. "Let's solve the mystery of how to untangle this big blob of wool."

"Aw," said Rocky. "I thought it was gonna be something big. Something good."

"Something scary," said Frank.

"Something interesting," said Jessica.

"Something *not* boring," said Amy.

"Or," said Judy, "we could play Jessica's level-three spelling game."

"I call yellow!" said Rocky, diving for some yellow wool.

"Brown!" said Frank, elbowing Rocky out of the way.

"Purple!" called Judy.

"Pink!" said Jessica, nudging Rocky.

Everybody pushed and shoved, trying to get to their favourite colour.

"Guess what? I know how to read colours," Amy told them when the ruckus died down. "My mum has a whole book about it."

"What does brown mean?" asked Frank.

"It means you're weird!" said Amy.

"Huh?"

"Just kidding. Most people pick blue for their favourite colour. Especially boys. But brown means you like nature, you're strong and people can count on you."

Frank held up one arm and flexed his muscles. "That's me. Ironman Pearl."

"Now me," said Rocky.

"Yellow. Yellow means you like the sun, you're cheerful and you have a good imagination."

"Cool," said Rocky.

"And you make babies cry."

"Huh?"

"Gotcha! Actually, yellow rooms do make babies cry more. Blue calms people down. And green helps you read better."

"Do pink!" said Jessica.

"Pink is the colour of love," said Amy.

"Ooh. Jessica's in love," Rocky teased.

"In love with spelling," said Frank.

"How about purple?" asked Judy.

"Purple is the colour of kings and queens and means you'll be rich. And you're creative."

"Sweet!" said Judy.

Stink poked his head into Judy's room. "Can I borrow five dollars?"

"I don't have five dollars."

"But you're gonna be rich, right?"

"Stink, I told you not to spy on me and my friends."

"Mum needs you downstairs… For a minute."

"Then hold this." Judy handed Stink her ball of wool. "I'll be right back," she said to her friends. But when she started downstairs, she could overhear Stink whispering with them.

Mum didn't need her. Stink had just made that up! Judy hurried back to her room. Everyone fell silent. Rocky poked Frank, who elbowed Amy. "You tell her," said Frank.

"Tell me what?" said Judy.

"We want you to take a test," said Amy.

"A test? What is this, school?"

"More like a quiz," said Rocky.

"An *alien* test," Stink said. "Like those magazine quizzes Mum's always taking."

"Think of it as a game," said Amy. She cleared her throat. "Ahem. First question. Do you like the colour green?"

"It's only my second favourite colour after purple. Why?"

"Do you eat MARS bars?" asked Rocky.

"I guess. Sometimes. Why are you asking that?"

"Do you wear sunglasses?" asked Jessica.

"When I'm at the beach, yeah. Why do you want to know?"

"Did you ever ride in a spaceship?" asked Frank.

"At Outer Space Land I did."

"Do you hold your breath when you pass a graveyard?" asked Stink.

"Doesn't everybody?"

"Do you ever answer a question with a question?" asked Frank.

"Huh?"

"See? I'm telling you," said Stink.

"Do you ever say, 'I come in peace'?" asked Amy.

"Nope."

"Yah-huh," said Stink. "When we were searching for Bigfoot you did."

"How many times have you seen the movie *E.T.*?" asked Rocky.

"Tons of times. But you guys have too, right?"

"Do you ever say 'Nanu Nanu'?"

"Nanu Nanu?"

"There! She just said it. That proves it," said Stink.

"Proves what? That I passed the test?"

"You passed all right," said Stink. "You are an alien. A for-real outer-space alien."

"Judy?" called Frank, peering at her through his glasses. "Are you in there?"

"Ring-a-ploopa wool-a-palooza yada-yada nanu-nanu," said Judy.

The room went dead quiet. Outer-space quiet. Nobody blinked. Amy looked at Frank, who looked at Rocky. Jessica popped up.

"Um, I just remembered ... I have to go," said Jessica. Amy nodded and got up too.

"Me too," said Rocky.

"Me three," said Frank, tripping over Amy and Rocky to get out of Judy's room as fast as he could.

Cheese Louise, thought Judy. *Try to be in a good mood, and your friends mistake you for an alien.*

Judy ran over to the open window.

"Hey, guys!" she called out. "I was just saying thanks! For helping me untangle the wool." But her friends were already halfway down the street, their backs to her.

Bad-Mood Itch

Pssst. Pssst. When Judy got to school the next morning, her friends (minus Amy, plus Jessica Finch) were whispering outside Class 3T. As soon as they saw Judy, they stopped. Since when were Rocky and Frank so palsy-walsy with Fink-Face Finch?

Oops. That wasn't good-mood thinking. WWJFD? What Would Jessica Finch Do? Judy tried to sound cheery. "Hey, guys. Happy Thursday!"

Frank waved. Jessica smiled. Rocky gave her a strange look. "We better get inside," he said. "Mr Todd already blinked the lights once."

It was so-not-working trying to be like Jessica Finch. Her friends just thought she was battier than Batgirl.

Mr Todd had tons of alarm clocks on his desk. "Three, two, one..." *BZZZZZZZ!* The clocks went off. Half the class jumped. The other half put their fingers in their ears.

"It's time!" Mr Todd smiled brightly. "Time to Measure Up! Today we begin our new maths unit. We're going to go the distance. We're going to have litres of fun. All day long we'll be measuring time and

space, our classroom and one another. Take out your maths books."

Judy did not even have to search her desk or her backpack. She pulled out her maths book from the top of the nice neat pile inside her desk.

"What are some tools we might use to measure things with?" Mr Todd asked.

Hannah raised her hand. "Ruler!"

Dylan raised his hand. "Yardstick!"

Jessica Finch raised her hand. "Measuring cup!"

Judy wanted to participate, just like Jessica Finch. "String!" Judy called out.

"Judy? Did you forget to raise your hand?" asked Mr Todd.

Oof. Judy stretched her hand in the air.

"Yes?" asked Mr Todd.

"I was going to say Elizabeth Black-well Women of Science ruler," said Judy, holding up her favourite ruler. "But some-body said ruler. So, I was thinking, you could measure something with a piece of string."

"Very good," said Mr Todd. "In ancient times, the length of your foot or the width of your thumb could be used to measure things."

Judy stuck her hand in the air again. "Mr Todd," she started, with her hand still raised. "Did you know that the longest guitar is more than eleven and a half metres? It says so right here on my Yardstick of Bubblegum box."

"Thank you, Judy. That's interesting."
He rolled the chalk in his hands. "But let's try not to interrupt."

"I raised my hand!" said Judy.

"That's a good start. But please wait to be called on." Mr Todd held up a jar of something that looked like rice. He wrote on the board: *1 inch = 3 grains of barley.*

Judy raised her hand again. Mr Todd peered over his glasses. "Yes, Judy?"

"The longest grain of rice is eight and a half millimetres, I'm pretty sure."

"She's like the Interrupting Chicken from that book," said Brody.

Judy's face got hot. Her ears turned as red as a turtle. A red-eared slider, that is.

"Let's all work on not interrupting,

Brody," said Mr Todd. He turned back to the board. "In old England, the king made a rule that if you took three grains of barley and put them end to end, that made an inch – or two and a half centimetres."

Judy could not help thinking about the world's longest rollercoaster and the world's longest moustache. She could not help thinking about the world's longest sandcastle and the world's longest banana split. She could not help wondering if the Yardstick of Bubblegum was the world's longest piece of bubblegum.

Judy shivered. She felt a chill. Probably the cold wind blowing in from the back of the room. Antarctica.

Snotsicles!

Judy sat on her hands. She did not want to be an Interrupting Chicken. And she did not want to take a zip, a trip or a skidoo to the Land of Snow and Ice, where her only friends would be nematodes.

At last, Class 3T got up and out of their seats. They scribbled estimates in their maths books. They measured the room in human feet. They measured Mr Todd's desk in thumbs. They measured their pencils in grains of barley.

"My pencil is twenty-two and a half barleys," said Frank, "counting the eraser." Class 3T figured out that Frank's pencil was almost nineteen centimetres.

They measured the length of Peanut the guinea pig, the distance from the pencil sharpener to the window and the time it took to walk-not-run from Class 3T to the principal's office and back.

They learned some way-cool measurements:

- George Washington's nose on Mount Rushmore: 6 metres long
- Statue of Liberty torch: nearly 4 metres long

@ Chesapeake Bay Bridge:

28,324 metres long

They found out that the United States was about 5,000 kilometres long and the distance from the earth to the sun was nearly 150 million kilometres!

"Great job today, class," said Mr Todd. "Tomorrow we'll measure things in hands, cubits and licks."

Judy raised her hand. She waited for Mr Todd to call on her. "Licks? Does that mean we get to eat ice cream?" she asked.

Mr Todd chuckled. "I'm afraid not. A lick is the distance from the tip of your thumb to the tip of your index finger when they're spread out like an *L*."

Judy's pencil was two and a quarter licks. Her Women of Science ruler was four licks. Her Yardstick of Bubblegum box was twelve licks.

"Over the weekend, think of something you'd like to measure, and come up with a unique way to measure it. On Monday, we're going to make our own rulers."

Rocky was going to measure his iguana, Houdini, using a pack of cards. Frank was going to measure his breakfast waffles in forks. Jessica Finch was going to measure the *Ultimate Speller's Dictionary* in Magic Straws.

"How about you, Judy? You're being super quiet," said Frank.

Judy itched. A bad-mood twitch. Remembering to raise her hand and not speak out in class and be like Jessica Finch all the time was making her jumpy. Trying to be in a good mood all the time was making her grumpy.

But she could not be a grumpa-lumpa-gus if she wanted to stay away from Antarctica. So she made a joke. "I'm going to measure my spaceship. You know, the one I flew in on with the Pod People from outer space."

Everybody half laughed.

"Kidding!" said Judy. "I'll probably measure Stink using sugar packets."

By the time Judy got home, she was in a tizzy. Her hair was frizzy and her brain was dizzy with bad-mood thoughts. *Grr.* She, Judy Moody, was in an almost mood. She checked her mood ring. It was awfully dark under there, where the purple nail polish was chipping off.

Judy had a heart-to-heart with Mouse. "This being in a good mood all the time sure is hard, Mouse. And my friends think I'm some kind of weirdo. I should just give up right now. Nobody would even know."

Mouse hid her eyes behind her paw. "You're right, Mouse. *I'd* know."

Mouse sniffled. Mouse sneezed. "I know, I know, Mouse. If I quit now, I might as

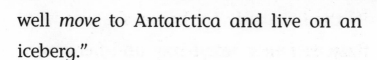

well *move* to Antarctica and live on an iceberg."

Judy picked up a ball of dark blue wool. *Knit, knit, knit. Loop-de-loop-de-loop.* At least she had wool to knit with again, thanks to her so-called not-alien friends. Her chain of finger knitting was getting longer and longer. It went down the stairs and around the banister and over the coat-stand and into the living-room, where it wound its way around the legs of the sofa.

The dark-blue ball of wool was used up in no time. Judy climbed up to her top bunk with a ball of purply wool. She cast off on her thumb.

Soon a lacy purple chain piled up in

her lap. Purple. The colour of kings and queens and creative ones. The colour of a mood ring painted *Joyful.*

Purple always put Judy in a better mood.

Suddenly, she had an idea. A royal idea. A plum of an idea. A lilac-lavender-NOT-aubergine idea. *Peanut Butter and Jam!* She, Judy Moody, would paint her same old chickenpox polka-dot wall purple. That way, at least her room would be in a good mood all the time. All she had to do now was ask the You-Know-Whos.

Judy found Mum downstairs playing Words With Frenemies on the computer. Dad was helping Stink with homework.

"Mum! Dad!" Judy begged. She got

down on her knees. "Please say yes. Pretty please with peanut-butter fingers on top?"

"Don't say yes," said Stink. "I bet she's going to ask you to take her to Fur and Fangs to get an Australian sugar glider or something."

"Or something," said Judy. "What even is a sugar glider?"

"It's like a flying squirrel with big bulgy eyes. From Australia. You can have one as a pet as long as you don't live in a four-syllable state."

"Huh?"

"You know. California, New Mexico,

Massachusetts and parts of Minnesota."

"Weird," said Judy.

"Well, we're not getting a flying sugar glider," said Mum. "Or any other Australian marsupial. So if that is the question, the answer is no."

"I'm not even asking for a sugar glider," said Judy.

"We're not going to say yes or no until we hear the question," said Dad.

"I was going to ask if we could paint my room. Maybe the wall behind my bunk beds? I was thinking purple."

"Why not?" said Mum.

"Sure," said Dad. "I have a bunch of colour samples in the garage. You pick out a colour, and we'll do it this weekend."

"Really? So that's a yes?" Judy asked. "Just like that?"

"Just like that," said Dad.

"You should have gone for the flying sugar glider," said Stink.

Sour Balls

On GMD No. 4, aka Friday, the finger-knitting chain followed Judy out the door and down the road and all the way to the bus stop!

"Look," said Stink. "You grew a tail!"

Judy turned to look. Sure enough, a tail of wool snaked down the pavement behind her. "Uh-oh. The end of my chain must have got caught on my backpack!" said Judy. "I've gotta go back."

"Hurry up or you'll miss the bus," said Stink.

Judy ran back to the house, gathering up the chain as she went. She tossed the whole thing inside the front door just as Mum and Dad were leaving. The chain looped over Dad's shoe and around his ankle. Dad shook his foot free.

"Judy. Mum and I want to talk to you about this knitting..."

"Late! Miss bus! Later! Bye!" Judy called back.

By the time Judy got back to the bus stop, her hair had escaped the kirby grips. She made two quick ponytails and asked, "Where's Rocky?"

"You know he always gets a ride when it rains," said Stink.

"But it's not raining."

"It's gonna. I like it when it rains. Rain means frogs."

"Can this day get any worse?" Judy asked.

"What do you mean?"

"Mum and Dad were having a knit fit. That's all."

"You're going to have to stop all that knitting stuff, aren't you?" Stink said.

"Never!"

"Yah-huh. I heard Mum and Dad talking."

"Don't pick a scab before it's time, Stink."

"Huh?"

"Never mind. Just tell me what they said."

"They said you're going to have to stop all that knitting stuff. They said it's taking over the whole house."

"No lie?"

"No lie."

"I can't stop now. I still have three more days to— I mean, if I stop now, I'll only have enough finger knitting to yarn bomb a birdhouse."

Judy could feel a snit fit coming on. A no-knit snit fit! She felt like stomping. But she could not stomp. She could not roar. She could not growl. Or even meow.

It was only Friday. She had to keep up her good-mood streak for three more days. That meant getting through one whole day of school without a Cheese-String Incident or an Interrupting Chicken Episode. Without even *thinking* that Jessica Finch was a fink-face. Otherwise, she'd be shivering in bunny boots and seeing sundogs from her own personal iceberg at the back of the room. Frostbite city!

But she'd made it this far, and Judy was determined, now more than ever, not to go anywhere *near* Antarctica. Not even close. Not even New Zealand.

She wiped the sour-ball look off her face. She put on a big fat fake smile.

She tried to sound smart and know-it-all,

like Jessica Finch. "When life gives you lemons, Stink, make lemonade." That's what grown-ups were always saying.

"Wha?"

"It's a saying. When life gives you sour balls, make sweet tarts."

"Huh?"

"When bad stuff happens, try to think of something good instead. Always look for the sweetness in the Sour Ball of Life."

"You sound like a birthday card," said Stink.

"Mum and Dad might make me stop finger knitting, right? That puts me in a bad mood. But they said I could paint my room this weekend. And that's a good thing."

Just then, a dark cloud passed over-
head. Judy heard a rumble of thunder.
All of a sudden, the sky opened up and it
started to pour.

Judy and Stink held their backpacks
over their heads. They dashed for cover.

"It's raining cats and dogs," Judy
wailed.

"It's raining toads and frogs," said Stink, grinning.

"Sour balls," said Judy.

"Don't you mean *sweet tarts*?" Stink said.

☙ ☙ ☙

It rained all morning. At indoor break in the gym, Judy took out the paint samples with funny names and passed them round.

"Rocky," said Judy. "You're not even looking."

"Why don't you just paint your room Martian Green," he suggested.

"Or Alien Orange," said Frank.

"Or Pluto Pink," said Jessica.

Judy did her best to ignore their alien

comments. "C'mon, you guys," she said. "Those aren't real colours." She fanned out the sample colours like a pack of cards.

"If it can't be Martian Green," said Rocky, "I'd have to pick Sunny-Side Up or Hay Is for Horses."

"Of course you'd pick yellow, Rock."

"I'd pick She Sells Seashells," said Amy.

"Blue is nice," said Judy.

"Statue of Liberty or Grass Stain," said Frank.

"No go. I'm not going to paint my room Grass Stain."

"Eraser, Tutu or Tippy Toes," said Jessica Finch.

"Those are all pink," said Judy. "How

about purple? There's Lav Out Loud, Plum Crazy, Peanut Butter and Jam or Saltwater Taffy."

Stink ran over from the second-grade side of the gym. "What colour do you like, Stink?" Judy asked him.

"Frog Prince," said Stink. "And Bullfrog and Ribbet and Pet Rock."

"You picked those because you like frogs."

"I know. Do they have Jawbreaker?"

"Jawbreaker is not a colour, Stink."

"Then I pick Snow Day."

"Snow Day is white," Judy grumped. "My whole room is already a Snow Day."

"Then how about Lemonade?" said Stink.

"Sorry. It looks like toad pee," said Judy. She shuffled her paint samples some more. At last, she put her favourite colour on top.

"Peanut Butter and Jam it is!"

Friday night was pizza-and-a-movie night. It was still raining outside. Judy leaned on her good-mood pillow and finger knitted between bites of cheesy pizza. She finger knitted her way through five tomato-red balls of wool while watching *The Cockroach that Ate Cleveland* with her family.

"How'd you like the movie?" Dad asked.

"They should call it *The Wool that Ate*

Cleveland," said Stink. "I couldn't see half the movie with Judy's finger knitting all over the TV."

Mum yawned. Stink yawned. Judy *yarned.* She kept knit-knit-knitting.

"Time for bed, kids," said Mum.

"But I'm not tired," said Judy. "One more skein of wool, please?"

"About the knitting," said Dad. "This wool is taking over the house. I trip over it everywhere I turn."

"It's driving Mouse crazy too," said Mum. She leaned over to untangle Mouse. "Poor cat. She looks like she's wearing a pink tutu."

"Did you hear what happened to the cat

that ate a ball of wool?" Stink asked.

Judy's eyes grew wide. "Woolly hairballs?"

"No. She had mittens!" said Stink. He cracked himself up.

Mum picked up a fuzzy pink section of the chain and peered at it. "Judy, is this ... Grandma Lou's hand-knitted dancing-mouse jumper I see in here?"

Judy stretched and let out a fake yawn-not-yarn. "It's late. I guess I better get to bed. Night, everyone."

"But I thought you weren't tired," said Stink.

"Mind your own knitting, Stink," said Judy. She gathered up her finger knitting and headed upstairs to bed.

"You can always count *dancing mice* if you can't get to sleep," Stink called after her.

In bed, Judy leaned on her frowny-face pillow and counted raindrops till she fell asleep.

Saltwater Taffy

On Saturday morning, Judy peered out the window. The rain had stopped! GMD No. 5 was off to a good start. Her mood pillow grinned at her. She picked up a coil of sun-yellow wool and soon her fingers were flying.

Dad went to get the paint for Judy's room. In the time he was gone, she finger knitted five whole balls of wool. Plum perfect!

Finally, Dad came home with the paint. "They were all out of Peanut Butter and Jam," said Dad.

Judy felt a twinge. Like a prickle, only worse. Bad-mood words like "No way!" and "So not fair!" shot through Judy's head, but she could not be in a bad mood for two more days. What a pickle.

She took a deep breath. "That's OK," she said calmly. "Peanut Butter and Jam is for babies."

"Hey! I love Peanut Butter and Jam," said Stink.

I rest my case, thought Judy, silently and to herself.

"Aren't you going to say, 'I rest my case' or something?" Stink asked.

"Or something."

"I got Saltwater Taffy instead," said Dad.

"Saltwater Taffy's good," said Judy. Dad snapped off the lid and Judy stirred the paint. She could hardly wait to dive in and slap some purple paint around.

"Saltwater Taffy?" Stink perked up. "Did you know that some guy had a sweetshop by the Atlantic Ocean like over a hundred years ago? One day, there was a big storm, the sea flooded his shop and the salt water got all over the sweets. And that's how it got invented and how come it's called saltwater taffy."

"I did not know that," said Judy. "You, little bother, I mean *brother*, are like a volcano – always spitting out interesting facts."

"Why are you being so nice?" asked Stink. "Mum! Judy's acting weird again."

"C'mon, you two," said Dad. "Let's get this party started."

"Stink's painting too?" Judy grumped, but then she caught herself. "Um, thanks for helping, Stinker. While we're getting ready, why don't you tell us how paint was invented?"

ⓐ   ⓐ   ⓐ

Before you could say "Saltwater Taffy" three times fast, Judy was dipping a roller in the paint tray. While Dad taped the edges, Judy slathered purple paint on the wall.

"Poiple!" she shouted with glee. Best-mood-ever purple! Purple was on-top-of-spaghetti royal.

Stink rolled paint on the wall. "Stink! You're splattering me," said Judy. She held out her T-shirt. "Human Spin Art."

"That's why we wore old T-shirts," said Dad, "and put down cardboard on the floor."

"Just don't get any paint on Hedda-Get-Betta, my Nancy Drew books, my finger knitting or—"

"Look," said Stink. "Mouse has one purple ear."

"You mean *purr*-ple." Judy cracked herself up. "She's going to have *two* purple ears, purple whiskers and a purple tail if she doesn't watch out. Scat, cat!" She shooed Mouse out of the room.

Stink cracked up. "You said scat. Scat is animal poo!"

In two shakes of a cat's tail, Judy and Stink had covered the wall in purple. Dad stood on a ladder to get all the edges. "How do you like your royal purple palace?" he asked.

Judy stepped back to admire their masterpiece. "Rare," she said.

"Now, we wait for this to dry. We may need a second coat," said Dad.

"You mean we have to do it all over again?" Judy asked. Oops. Bad-mood words. "You mean we *get* to do this all over again?" She turned on a smile.

"We'll see. In the meantime, I'm going to rinse these rollers and brushes out."

Judy picked up her finger knitting. Stink sat cross-legged next to her. He stared at the wall. He stared sideways. He stared upside down.

"Watching paint dry is snore pie," said Stink.

"It's not *so* boring," said good-mood Judy.

Stink stared at the wall some more. "Did you know in India they have a purple frog? Also called a doughnut frog."

"I did not know that," said Judy. "Did you know purple is the colour of kings and queens?"

"I knew that. Did you know Klingons have purple blood in the sixth Star Trek movie? And Mace Windu is the only Jedi with a purple light saber?"

"I did not know that," said Judy. "Did you know nothing rhymes with purple?"

"Ya-huh! *Urple. Flurple. Snurple.*"

"Use one of those in a sentence, Stink."

"My name is *Urple* from the planet *Flurple* and I like to drink *Snurple*."

"Ha ha. Now who's the alien?" said Judy.

"Know any more purple facts?" Stink asked. "I'm all out."

Judy scratched her head. She looped sky-blue wool over her finger and back again. "Purple-o-phobia is fear of the colour purple."

"Is not," said Stink. "You made that up."

"You'll never know."

Stink couldn't sit still. He danced and pranced around the room, singing into a paintbrush all about a crazy one-eyed, one-horned, flying purple people eater.

Judy pranced around with him, singing into her hairbrush. She didn't know all the words, so she just made stuff up.

"Beep, beep, boo bop bop, walla walla Washington!" Judy sang.

"That's not even in the song," said Stink.

"So?" They cracked up some more. "Beep, beep, boo bop bop..." On the last *walla walla*, Stink's foot got caught in the finger knitting. He stumbled back a step. He stumbled right smack-dab into the brand-new wall of purple paint.

The tail end of Judy's finger knitting was floating in the paint tray. "Sorry." Stink crawled over and plucked the chain out of the paint. "It'll dry. This part will just be Saltwater Taffy purple."

SPLAT!

Judy was seeing purple. She stared at the freshly painted wall. Her mouth hung open. "Stink! That's your butt on my new wall!"

"Just my butt *print*," said Stink.

Judy felt a door slam coming on. But she had made a promise to herself. *No bad moods!* She couldn't let herself slam the door to so much as her pencil case.

Mum and Dad came rushing upstairs. "We heard a crash," said Mum. "Is everything OK up here?"

"Everything but my new wall," said Judy.

"What happened?" asked Dad, looking at the big double smudge mark.

"Stink got his butt on my new wall, that's what. And he wrecked my finger knitting." Judy's eyes smarted. She forgot all about her good-mood streak.

"We were singing 'Purple People Eater'," said Stink. "Judy too. Then I tripped on Judy's knitting."

"Judy," said Mum. "What did we tell you about all the finger knitting everywhere?"

Judy stared at her shoe through watery eyes.

"This is what happens when—" Mum started.

"But it's Stink's fault. I was just trying to be in a good mood. Honest."

"We're not saying you have to stop," Mum said. "We're just saying we can't have a trail of knitting all over the place, in every room of the house."

"Yeah, it's like longer than the Great Wall of China," said Stink.

"Stink, you're not helping," said Dad.

"This can't go on, honey."

"Mum's right," said Dad.

"But..." Judy's eyes welled up.

"Tell you what," said Dad. "Let's let the wall dry overnight. But starting tomorrow, all the wool stays in your wardrobe."

"Why is *she* crying?" Stink asked. "I'm the one with a purple butt." He wiggled his behind. He leapfrogged across the floor. "I'm a purple doughnut frog! Ribbet!" Mum and Dad couldn't help laughing. Even Judy cracked up a little.

"Don't worry about the wall," said Dad. "A second coat will cover it right up."

After Mum and Dad left, Stink ran over to his room and came back with a zombie. One that Grandma Lou had knitted for him. "Here," said Stink. "You can unwind it and use the wool. Maybe you'll feel better if you keep finger knitting."

"You'd give up a zombie for me?" said Judy. "Thanks!" She looped the end over her thumb. *Knit, knit, knitknitknit.*

"You're fast!" said Stink.

"I'm a Knit Wit!"

"You could win the Finger-Knitting Olympics."

"Think so?"

"I know so. They'd give you a big gold trophy called the Golden Needle and you'd be all famous and get your picture on a cereal box and everything. Mum and Dad would be all proud and we'd live happily ever after in a house made of money."

"OK, but it's *finger* knitting, Stink.

So instead of the Golden Needle trophy, don't you mean the Golden *Finger* trophy?"

"Good one," said Stink.

Purple People Eater

That night, Judy had a sleepover with Mouse on the downstairs sofa, because:

1. Her room was stinky. (Not as in Stink, but as in new-paint smell.)
2. She did not want Stink's butt print to haunt her in the middle of the night.
3. Stink's room was out because Stink snored.

The next morning, she stumbled up the stairs, half awake. Judy followed the chain of knitting down the hall to the bathroom. The door was closed. The finger-knitting chain stretched under the door.

Judy knocked on the bathroom door. "Hey, Stinker!"

"Hey, what?" Stink said, coming up right behind her.

Judy jumped. "Wait. You're out here? Then who? I thought you were in there."

"I thought *you* were in there."

"So who's in the bathroom?"

Stink shrugged. "Mum and Dad aren't up yet. Hey, I know. Maybe a finger-knitting freak-o-maniac broke in to steal your world-record finger-knitting chain."

"Get a clew." Judy creaked open the

door. The finger-knitting chain wormed its way across the floor. The end dangled smack-dab in the middle of … the toilet.

"Eeww!" said Judy. "It's in the toilet water."

"P.U.," said Stink, pinching his nose.

With Stink's brand-new toothbrush, Judy lifted up the chain of knitting and

wiggled it at Stink. "Wet yeti tail!" she cried.

"Uck! Cooties! Get that thing away from me." Stink ducked and dodged the wet wool. "And throw away my toothbrush."

Judy chased Stink with the wet wool into her room. That's where they found Mouse stalking and hunting her prey – a clew of finger knitting. She pounced on it, picked it up with her paw and started to chew.

Their eyes followed the knitting chain around the room. It dangled over the wardrobe door, snaked across the book-shelves, looped around Judy's Krazy Kat Klock and dropped down onto her desk.

A clump of wool was caught in the Venus flytrap's trap. "Give it up, Jaws," said Judy. "This isn't a dead fly, you know." She eased the wool out of the trap. "I think our finger-knitting freak-o-maniac is a *feline* freak-o-maniac," said Judy.

Stink cracked up.

"Hold out your hands, Stink," Judy said. "Take this end of the wool."

"Eeww! The cootie end? No way."

"Pretty please with silver-dollar pancakes on top? You owe me." Judy pointed to Stink's butt print on her new purple wall.

"No way am I touching wool that's full of toilet cooties."

"Then help me find the other end of the chain downstairs," said Judy. She led the way. Mouse bounded after them.

The living-room was a spider's web of wool. The sofa was a nest of finger knitting. The coffee table looked like a plate of spaghetti. Wool twisted like a tornado around the room and hung like rainbow-coloured cobwebs from the ceiling light.

"Mouse did all this?" Stink asked.

"Tell me about it. She yarn bombed the living-room. C'mon, Stink. Help me pick up all this wool and get it up to my room before Mum and Dad wake up."

"Not possible."

"If we do it really fast, it can be like a

race." So Judy and Stink started to scoop up piles of wool. Heaps of wool. Loads of wool. Mountains of wool.

Stink got his feet tangled in wool. He got his head tangled in wool. He got his middle tangled in wool. He even had a wool moustache. "Revenge of Yarnzilla!" he croaked, pretending to be a zombie.

"You look like a mummy," said Judy.

"Look! Mouse is a mummy too," said Stink. "A cat mummy! Did you know that in ancient Egypt they even had hippo mummies, not just cat ones?"

"Not now, Stink-o-pedia."

Judy tried to unwrap the wool from around Stink Mummy's ankles.

"I think the wool is winning the race," said Stink. "Wool: One. Us: Zero."

"I have an idea." Judy found the other end of the finger-knitting chain on the coat-stand. "We start with one end and wind it up into one big giant ball."

"Genius," said Stink.

Judy held the end in her fingers and wound the chain around and around until it had formed a tiny ball. Soon it was the size of a golf ball. Judy kept winding while Stink fed the chain to her, untangling knots and snags and tangles as he went.

"Faster, Stink. Faster!" In no time, the ball of wool was as big as a tennis ball. Then it was as big as a softball.

"This is bigger than my Jawbreaker of Doom," said Stink.

By the time Mum and Dad got up, Judy and Stink had a finger-knitting ball the size of a football. A basketball. A beach-ball.

"Creative idea," said Mum.

"Keep it up," said Dad.

"Wrap and roll!" said Judy.

Judy and Stink followed the chain into the kitchen, up the stairs, down the hall, into the bathroom, out of the bathroom and into Judy's room, winding and winding with every step.

Yellow wool was rolled into the ball. Purple wool. Blue and red and key-lime green and atomic-tangerine wool. Even fuzzy-wuzzy, space-dyed wool was rolled into the great big ball. They wrapped and rolled until every bit of Judy's finger-knitting chain went into the ginormous ball.

"I bet we just rolled up ten kilometres of wool," said Stink. "No, twenty. No, fifty. This thing must weigh half as much as me."

"Wow!" said Mum. "Finger-knittin' good!"

"Wow!" said Dad. "That's one big ball of wool."

"Stink, I think we got a clew," said Judy. Everybody laughed.

"It's as big as Pluto!" said Stink. "It could be a dwarf planet. The Purple Urple!"

"Let's roll Purple Urple upstairs to my room," said Judy.

Judy and Stink stood back to admire the giant ball of finger knitting. Peeks of pink and glimpses of green shone through the purple on top.

"It's like the world's longest rainbow," said Judy.

"The Fuzzy Wuzzy that Ate Frog Neck Lake!" said Stink.

"I'm going to name it the Purple People Eater," said Judy.

"You definitely should win the world record for the Purple People Eater. To go with your gold medal in the Finger-Knitting Olympics."

Judy looked at Stink. Stink looked at Judy. They picked up their air guitars. Stink started dancing around. They sang the one-eyed, one-horned, flying purple people eater song again. *Beep, beep, boo bop bop, walla walla Washington!*

Later that night, Judy propped her elbows on her good-mood pillow and eyeballed the Purple People Eater. It was purple, all right. But it was also Roy G. Biv. **R**ed, **O**range, **Y**ellow, **G**reen, **B**lue, **I**ndigo and **V**iolet.

All the colours of her many moods.

Judy took out a marker. *Brainwave!* She turned Stink's butt print into two funny faces. One side was a bad-mood face. The other was a good-mood face.

Judy knitted her brow. She had just barely made it through GMD No. 6. All week long, she'd played keep-away with bad moods. Finger knitting had helped her stay in a good mood. *That* was something to be happy about. But tomorrow was

Monday. GMD No. 7. Would she, could she make it?

Eureka! She, Judy Moody, had a moon-tastic idea. The perfect way to celebrate Good Mood Day No. 7. And to brighten up a boring old Monday.

Judy Un-Moody

It bumped down the stairs. It thumped across the living-room. And with a whoosh, a push and a smoosh, the big bright ball of wool rolled out the front door.

The Purple People Eater was going to school!

At last, it was Good Mood Day No. 7 and she, Judy Moody, could not wait to get to school. She was in a mood. A good mood. She even forgot to put her hair in ponytails or match her clothes or put on lip gloss or finish her homework.

Judy and Stink rolled the giant ball of finger knitting down the road, over tree-root bumps, past Super-Postman Jack Frost and around the corner till ... the big ball of wool got away from them.

"Aagh! Runaway Purple People Eater!" yelled Judy. They ran after it.

"Stop! Stop that ball." Just then, it hit a stop sign.

"Phew! That was a close one," said Judy.

The bus doors opened. *Oomph!* Judy

lugged the giant ball up the steps of the bus. Kids *ooh*ed and *ahh*ed, but Judy's friends were not on the bus.

"Who's your friend?" asked the bus driver.

"The Purple People Eater," said Judy. "It's for Mr Todd's class. I'm going to surprise my teacher."

"I bet he'll be surprised, all right," said the driver.

☺   ☺   ☺

When Judy got to school, she gave the Purple People Eater an extra-big push through the front doors. *Wheee!* It rolled across the front lobby. A kindergartener jumped out of the way. It started down the hall. The big ball was stopped by a ... foot.

Not a Bigfoot foot. A grown-up foot in a low-heeled sensible shoe.

The principal!

"What on earth!" said Ms Tuxedo. She looked up and saw Judy. "Judy Moody. I might have known," she teased. "What is it this time? A planet? An art project? A new game for Physical Education?"

"I'm going to surprise Mr Todd," said Judy. "It's for maths class!" She told the principal all about finger knitting and her moods and their Measure Up! unit in maths.

"I don't think this is going to fit in your locker or your desk, do you?"

"No way," said Judy.

"Tell you what. Let's roll it into my

office, and we'll hide it there until you're ready. What time is maths class?"

"One forty-five," said Judy.

"One forty-five it is! It'll be our secret."

"Rare!" said Judy. "Thanks."

Judy practically skipped down the hall to class, humming the Purple People Eater song. She spotted her friends in a huddle outside Rocky's locker. She rushed up to them. "Guys! Guys! Why weren't you on the bus today?"

Frank's eyes got big. Amy took a step back. Jessica pointed to the sign they were making for Rocky's locker. "Alien-Free Zone," said Rocky.

Judy held two fingers in the air for a joke. "I come in peace!"

Her friends just stared at her.

"You guys, I am NOT an alien, OK? Yes, I might like green and, yes, I've been known to eat a MARS bar and watch *E.T.*, but I'm still me. Honest! Cross my heart and hope to spy."

Judy turned and headed to class. Pencils and erasers and rulers went flying out of her backpack. But she did not care. She did not stop to pick them up.

All morning, Judy tried not to let a bad mood ruin GMD No. 7. If only it were time for maths class. She watched the clock. Had it gone backwards? Nine more minutes of subject-verb agreement and counting.

Finally, the loudspeaker crackled. "Judy Moody to the principal's office. Judy

Moody? Please come to the front office."

Getting called to the front office meant one thing, and one thing only. *T* is for T-R-O-U-B-L-E. That was one word that did *not* agree with its subject – Judy.

Luckily, Judy wasn't in trouble today. But Class 3T did not know that. They stared and glared at her like she had just landed from outer space.

Mr Todd nodded. Judy got up out of her seat, trying to look un-guilty. When she got to the office, Ms Tuxedo looked up and down the hall like a super spy.

"The coast is clear," she whispered. "Ready?"

"Ready, Freddy," said Judy.

The principal pointed to the Purple

People Eater. "Let's roll on down to maths class and Measure Up!"

Ms Tuxedo and Judy roll-roll-rolled the ball as gently as they could down the hall. They stopped outside Class 3T. One, two, three … and they both gave a push. The Purple People Eater zoomed through the doorway and into Class 3T, rolling right smack-dab into Mr Todd's desk.

"Ack!" Mr Todd jumped back.

"Surprise!" Judy shouted.

"What have we here?" asked her teacher. "The World's Biggest Super-Ball?"

"Judy Moody brought something to liven up maths class," Ms Tuxedo explained. "I offered to keep it for her until then so it would be a surprise."

Mr Todd pretended to grunt and groan as he helped Judy lift it up onto the desk.

"Ooh. Eee. Ooh. Ahh. Ahh," everybody exclaimed.

"It's like a planet!" said Rocky.

"Planet Moody," said Frank.

Judy tilted it left and right. She rolled it back and forth for the class to see. The gigantic ball of finger knitting dazzled with all the colours of the rainbow.

"Judy?" asked Mr Todd. "Do you want to tell us about this?"

"This is my finger-knitting chain," said Judy.

"You knitted that whole entire thing?" Jessica asked.

"Whoa!"

"Weird!"

"Crazy!"

"Awesome!"

"OK. So. Yes. It all started with Backwards Day. I was in a good mood all day. It was way-super fun and Mr Todd and Ms Tuxedo and everybody thought it was great, right? So I decided then and there to give myself the ultimate test – I would try to be in a good mood for ONE WHOLE WEEK."

"That would be a challenge for any of us," said Mr Todd. Ms Tuxedo nodded.

"I had to do something to help me get through the week or I'd go cuckoo-for-coconuts. I started finger knitting like crazy. Then I realized it helped take my mind off the bad moods."

"Good for you," said Mr Todd.

"Whoa. You must have knitted your fingers off," said Frank.

"A skein a day keeps the bad moods away!" Judy joked.

"That's a new one to me." Ms Tuxedo laughed.

"There's lots of purple in here because it's my favourite colour. So I call it the Purple People Eater," said Judy. "But there's also sky blue and grass green and fuzzy gold and tomato red and periwinkle. I guess you could say it's kind of like a giant mood ring. The colours are all my different moods."

"Well, class, we all have lots of moods, but as your teacher, I do appreciate bringing *good* moods to our classroom."

"How did you ever get it to be so long?" Jessica asked.

"I just kept adding colours and it got longer and longer and longer and pretty soon it started to eat up the whole house. My mum and dad weren't too happy – so I rolled the chain into a big giant ball."

"Class," said Mr Todd, "anybody want to take a guess at how long it is?"

"I bet it's as long as the Chesapeake Bay Bridge!" said Hunter.

"That's almost thirty kilometres long," said Rocky.

"I bet it could go all the way across the United States," said Frank.

"Nah-uh. That's about five thousand kilometres," said Jessica.

The classroom buzzed with excitement. "I bet it could stretch from here to the moon," said Hannah.

"I think we're getting a little carried away here," Mr Todd said. Then he went over and whispered something in Ms Tuxedo's ear. She nodded. "Class 3T," he said. "We're taking maths class outside. Grab your rulers and maths books, and follow Ms Tuxedo. I'll meet you out the front."

❀ ❀ ❀

Class 3T waited with Ms Tuxedo on the pavement in front of the school. Mr Todd drove up in his Mini.

"Where are we going?" some kids asked.

"Field trip!"

"No way are we all going to fit in there," said Rocky.

Mr Todd hopped out. "We're staying right here," he said. "Let's start by using Judy's chain to figure out one car length." In no time, he had Class 3T unwinding Judy's finger-knitting chain. They measured and multiplied and made notes.

"Mr Todd," said Judy. "Can we yarn bomb your Mini?"

"Excuse me?" said Mr Todd.

"Yarn bomb?" said Ms Tuxedo.

"It's a real thing," said Judy. "You wrap something like a tree or a car or a flag-pole in knitting. It's way cool. And it's art!"

"I see," said Ms Tuxedo.

Mr Todd studied his car. He studied the big ball of wool. "Here's an idea. How about if we wrap the chain around the car, and estimate how many times it might go round?"

"Yippee!" yelled the third graders. Around and around they went, wrapping Mr Todd's car in all the colours of the rainbow. They went around one time, five times, ten times, a hundred, singing the one-eyed, one-horned, flying purple people eater song the whole time. Ms Tuxedo knew words to the song that Judy had never heard.

They wrapped the wool around Mr Todd's car one hundred and fifty-one and a half times until the car was a crazy quilt of colours.

The kids in Class 3T were maths magicians. They measured the chain once around Mr Todd's car: eleven metres! They multiplied that by the number of times it went around the car. They figured out that Judy's finger-knitting chain was 1,666.5 metres long. As in over one kilometre long.

As in 166,650 centimetres to be exact! As in 2,651 steps. As in 20,150 licks!

Judy stood back to admire their work of art. One thing was for sure and absolute positive – Judy's moods brought colour to the world. Greens for energetic moods, yellows for sunshiny stay-away-from-Antarctica moods, blues for calm moods and purples for royal on-top-of-spaghetti moods.

By the time they had finished, Judy's hair was wild and woolly. She did *not* look like Jessica same-same Finch. She looked like a Human Yarn Bomb – covered in flecks of fuzzy wool from head to toe.

But she sure felt a lot smarter than she had a week ago. Not just maths smarts.

Mood smarts. If ever Judy felt a world-record bad mood coming on, she knew just what to do. She, Judy Moody, could finger knit away the blues.

"This *is* a work of art," said Ms Tuxedo, snapping a picture of Class 3T with their creation.

"Ms Tuxedo," said Judy. "You know how we can have a school photo do-over? Do you think I could get mine taken with the Purple People Eater?"

"I don't see why not." Ms Tuxedo winked at Judy. "Class 3T," she said, "I have to say this is the most creative maths I've seen in all my years as principal of Virginia Dare School."

"Let's give ourselves a POTB!" Mr Todd said. Class 3T gave themselves a big Pat On The Back.

Amy Namey's class came outside to have a look. They *ooh*ed and *aah*ed.

"Only Judy Moody could finger knit a chain of wool over a kilometre long!" said Rocky. "That's fifteen whole football pitches!"

"Only Judy Moody could make maths this fun," said Frank.

"Only Judy Moody," agreed Amy. Jessica Finch nodded. Everybody whooped and clapped and woo-hooed for Judy.

She sat down on the kerb. It sure felt good to be the regular, all-moods Judy

Moody again. Her friends huddled around her. "Sorry we thought you were an alien," said Frank.

"I didn't think she was an alien," said Jessica Finch.

"Did too," said Frank and Amy.

"Not so fast," said Rocky. "Are we one-hundred-per-cent for sure she's *not* an alien?" Rocky whispered to the others, then turned to Judy. "Name one thing Judy Moody likes to collect," he said to her.

"ABC gum," said Judy.

"Too easy," said Amy. "When is Judy's birthday?"

"April the first. April Fools' Day!"

"Who is the president of the United States?" asked Frank.

"How's knowing that going to prove I'm the real Judy?" asked Judy.

"What was the wackiest, best Judy Moody idea ever?" Rocky asked.

"Making the Purple People Eater?" Judy said.

"Let's vote," said Rocky. "Who thinks she's the real Judy Moody?" Four hands shot up in the air. "Will the real Judy Moody please stand up!"

The not-so-moody Judy stood up. She stood next to Class 3T's work of maths art. Her face was a mile of smile. She was happy as Larry. Happy as a hermit crab. Happy as a clam and an exclamation mark!

One by one, Frank handed her the

stuff she had dropped in the corridor earlier that morning – the Yardstick of Bubblegum box, her Women of Science ruler, three guinea pig erasers and one Grouchy pencil.

"Welcome back," said Frank.

Beep, beep, boo bop bop, walla walla Washington!

photo by Michele McDonald

Megan McDonald is the author of the popular Judy Moody and Stink series, as well as the Judy Moody and Friends series for new readers. She has written many other books for children, including the Ant and Honey Bee stories, the Sisters Club series and several picture books. Before she began writing full-time, Megan McDonald worked as a librarian, a bookseller and a living-history actress. She lives in Northern California with her husband, Richard Haynes, who is also a writer.

Peter H. Reynolds is the illustrator of the popular Judy Moody and Stink series in addition to many other books, including several for

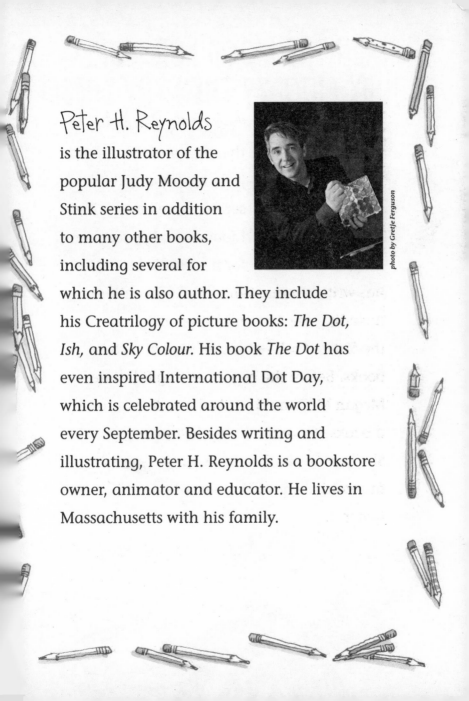

which he is also author. They include his Creatrilogy of picture books: *The Dot, Ish,* and *Sky Colour.* His book *The Dot* has even inspired International Dot Day, which is celebrated around the world every September. Besides writing and illustrating, Peter H. Reynolds is a bookstore owner, animator and educator. He lives in Massachusetts with his family.

IN THE MOOD FOR MORE JUDY MOODY? THEN TRY THESE!

MEGAN McDONALD
illustrated by Peter H. Reynolds
JUDY MOODY
AROUND THE WORLD IN 8½ DAYS
Ciao!

MEGAN McDONALD
illustrated by Peter H. Reynolds
JUDY MOODY GOES TO COLLEGE
Genius!

MEGAN McDONALD
illustrated by Peter H. Reynolds
JUDY MOODY GIRL DETECTIVE
Crumbs!

MEGAN McDONALD
illustrated by Peter H. Reynolds
JUDY MOODY AND THE NOT BUMMER SUMMER
Thrill-a-delic!
BIG FOOT CLUB

MEGAN McDONALD
illustrated by Peter H. Reynolds
JUDY MOODY AND THE BAD LUCK CHARM
Whoa!

MEGAN McDONALD
illustrated by Peter H. Reynolds
JUDY MOODY MOOD MARTIAN
loop-de-loop!

MEGAN McDONALD
illustrated by Peter H. Reynolds
JUDY MOODY AND THE BUCKET LIST
1-2-3, wheee!

Have
you
met
Stink?

Meet Stink, Judy Moody's little "bother,"
er, brother. <u>Very</u> little brother...

Stink was short. Short, shorter, shortest.
Stink was an inchworm. Short as a ...
stinkbug!

Stink was the shortest one in the
Moody family (except for Mouse, the cat).
The shortest second-grader in Class 2D.
Probably the shortest human being in the
whole world, *including Alaska and Hawaii*.
Stink was one whole head shorter than
his sister, Judy Moody. Every morning
he made Judy measure him. And every
morning it was the same.

One metre, twelve centimetres tall.
Shrimpsville.

Excerpt from *Stink: The Incredible Shrinking Kid*

MEET JUDY MOODY'S BROTHER STINK!

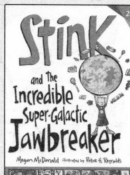

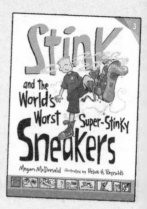

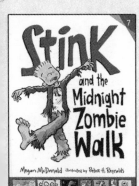

Stink and the Midnight Zombie Walk

Megan McDonald illustrated by Peter H. Reynolds

Stink and the Freaky Frog Freakout

Megan McDonald illustrated by Peter H. Reynolds

Stink and the Shark Sleepover

Megan McDonald illustrated by Peter H. Reynolds

Stink and the Attack of the Slime Mould

Megan McDonald illustrated by Peter H. Reynolds

Stink Hamlet and Cheese

Megan McDonald illustrated by Peter H. Reynolds

Stink-o-pedia

SUPER STINK-Y STUFF FROM A to Z

Megan McDonald illustrated by Peter H. Reynolds

Stink-o-pedia 2

MORE STINK-Y STUFF FROM A to Z

Megan McDonald illustrated by Peter H. Reynolds

JUDY MOODY AND STINK
ARE STARRING TOGETHER!

In full colour!